Dear Parent:

Congratulations! Your child is taking the first steps on an exciting journey. The destination? Independent reading!

STEP INTO READING® will help your child get there. The program offers five steps to reading success. Each step includes fun stories and colorful art. There are also Step into Reading Sticker Books, Step into Reading Math Readers, Step into Reading Write-In Readers, Step into Reading Phonics Readers, and Step into Reading Phonics First Steps! Boxed Sets—a complete literacy program with something for every child.

Learning to Read, Step by Step!

Ready to Read Preschool–Kindergarten
• big type and easy words • rhyme and rhythm • picture clues
For children who know the alphabet and are eager to begin reading.

Reading with Help Preschool–Grade 1
• basic vocabulary • short sentences • simple stories
For children who recognize familiar words and sound out new words with help.

Reading on Your Own Grades 1–3
• engaging characters • easy-to-follow plots • popular topics
For children who are ready to read on their own.

Reading Paragraphs Grades 2–3
• challenging vocabulary • short paragraphs • exciting stories
For newly independent readers who read simple sentences with confidence.

Ready for Chapters Grades 2–4
• chapters • longer paragraphs • full-color art
For children who want to take the plunge into chapter books but still like colorful pictures.

STEP INTO READING® is designed to give every child a successful reading experience. The grade levels are only guides. Children can progress through the steps at their own speed, developing confidence in their reading, no matter what their grade.

Remember, a lifetime love of reading starts with a single step!

W9-BON-053

For Kimi Havelka
—J.H.

Text copyright © 2009 by Joan Holub
Illustrations copyright © 2009 by Tim Bowers

Library of Congress Cataloging-in-Publication Data
Holub, Joan.
Shampoodle / by Joan Holub ; illustrated by Tim Bowers. — 1st ed.
  p. cm. — (Step into reading. A step 2 book)
Summary: Rhyming text describes a dog grooming establishment on picture day and the uproar some curious kittens cause when they try to explore.
ISBN 978-0-375-85576-4 (trade) — ISBN 978-0-375-95576-1 (lib. bdg.)
[1. Stories in rhyme. 2. Grooming—Fiction. 3. Dogs—Fiction. 4. Animals—Infancy—Fiction. 5. Cats—Fiction.] I. Bowers, Tim, ill. II. Title.
PZ8.3.H74Sh 2009
[E]—dc22 2008035185

Printed in the United States of America

10 9 8 7 6 5 4 3

Shampoodle

by Joan Holub

illustrated by Tim Bowers

Random House New York

At the park,
it's picture day.
Dogs need grooming
right away.

5

6

We do dog-dos.

Come and see.

Clean and shiny.

Not one flea.

7

Barking. Bouncing.

Dogs trot in.

Sniffing. Snuffling.

Let's begin!

Pushing buttons.

Zooming up.

Spinning. Twirling.

Dizzy pup.

9

Scrubbing. Bubbling.

No! Don't shake!

Dogs won't listen.

Big mistake.

Rubbing. Patting.

Fluffy towel.

Tangling. Combing.

Puppies howl.

11

Nosy kitties.

Out for fun.

Puppies spot them.

Run, cats, run!

Chasing. Racing.

In the shop.

Hoses spraying.

Stop, dogs, stop!

Slipping. Tripping.

Lots of goo.

Dogs go sliding

in shampoo.

Dripping poodle.

Pug half-styled.

Soggy sheepdog.

Running wild.

Groomer grooming
gets a fright.
Rollers. Curlers.
Tugged too tight!

Groomer snipping
gets a scare.
Dogs end up
with wacky hair.

Hissing. Yowling.

What a spat!

Out the pet door.

Cats all scat.

Squeak toys.

Snack treats.

Slobber. Drool.

Good dogs. Sit. Stay.

That's the rule!

Pups are pooped out.
They all rest.
Time to make them
look their best.

Cutting. Drying.
Warm air blast.
Styling. Braiding.
Done at last.

New hair. Blue hair.

Beads with knots.

Purple hair
with polka dots.

26

Spiked hair. Mohawk.

Striped like skunk.

Glitter critter.

Super funk.

Picture time now.

Off they go.

Dogs dash out
with kids in tow.

PUP Pictures TODAY

30

Happy! Yappy!

Pups collide.

Splish-splash!

Uh-oh! Dog mud slide!

31